caillou®

And The Big Slide

Adaptation: Chouette Publishing
Text: Jeannine Beaulieu
Illustrations: Taken from the animated series and adapted by Les Studios de la Souris Mécanique

chouette   COOKIE JAR

Caillou and his daddy were spending the

afternoon at the playground. Caillou loved the

 , especially when Daddy pushed.

swing

"Higher, Daddy, higher!" Caillou shouted.

From his swing, Caillou saw Clementine.

Caillou loved playing with Clementine.

Whenever they played on the  ,

train

she let him be the engineer.

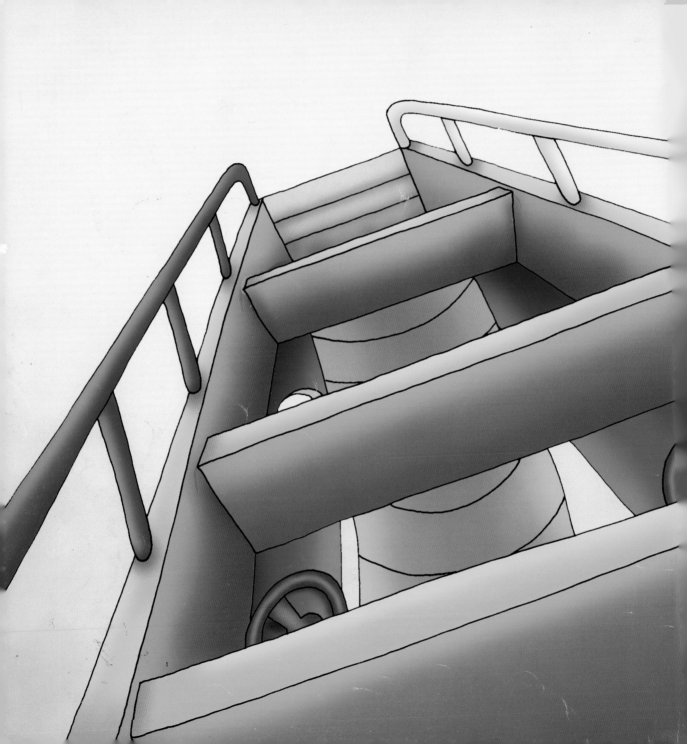

"Let's go down the slide," Clementine

suggested. "Let's go down the big  .

slide

It's much more fun."

Caillou and ran over to the big

Clementine

kids' area. Caillou stopped in front of the

slide and stared up in surprise. It looked so

high! Caillou was afraid to climb up.

Caillou looked around the playground

and saw the play tunnels. The large,

brightly colored  didn't look

tube

nearly as scary.

"Let's play in the tunnels first,"

Caillou

suggested.

"Okay," said Clementine. "Try and

catch me."

Daddy was sitting on a

bench

watching Caillou and Clementine play.

"Caillou, we'll have to go home soon,"

Daddy said, looking at his .

watch

"Let's go down the slide," Clementine said.

"You first," Caillou said.

 climbed up and pushed herself off

Clementine

at the top and was at the bottom before she

had time to shout "whee"!

"That was fun!" she exclaimed. "Now it's

your turn."

"Okay, okay,"  mumbled.

Caillou

Caillou climbed up slowly, clinging to the
 and repeating, "I'm not scared.

handles

I'm not scared."

But when he reached the top, he was

shaking with fear. Clementine looked very

small to him, way down at the bottom of

the . He could hardly hear her

slide

shouting, "Slide, Caillou! Slide!"

Caillou was terrified. He couldn't move.

"Daddy, !" he cried.

Daddy

Clementine told Caillou's daddy, "I think

Caillou's scared. I wasn't scared a bit,"

she said.

"You're a big , Clementine. You

girl

can do lots of things."

Daddy climbed the  .

ladder

"Hmm, this slide is pretty high, isn't it?"

Caillou nodded.

"I know what we can do, Caillou. Let's go

down together. It'll be fun, you'll see."

Daddy held Caillou's .

hand

"Are you ready, Caillou?"

"Ready, Daddy."

" 1 , 2 , three, here we go!"
One   two

Caillou was thrilled.

"Did you see that, Clementine? I came down

the big slide!"

"I came down all by myself," she told him.

"So can I,"  insisted. "I'm not

Caillou

scared anymore."

Caillou climbed back up and whizzed down

the slide, shouting, "Look at me-e-e-e!"

"Good for you, Caillou," said.

Daddy

"I'm proud of you! You're a big boy."

"It's time to go  now."

home

"Just one more time, please, Daddy!"

Caillou ran back to the ladder with

Clementine close behind.

One, two, 3 , whee! And of course,

three

that wasn't the last "one more time"!

Adaptation of text by Jeannine Beaulieu based on the screenplay of the CAILLOU animated film series produced by Cookie Jar Entertainment Inc. (© 1997 CINAR Productions (2004) Inc., a subsidiary of Cookie Jar Entertainment Inc.).
All rights reserved.
Original script written by Christel Kleitch.
Illustrations taken from the animated television series and adapted by Les Studios de la Souris Mécanique.
Art Director: Monique Dupras

Bibliothèque et Archives nationales du Québec and Library and Archives Canada cataloguing in publication data
Beaulieu, Jeannine, 1934-
Caillou and the big slide
(Abracadabra)
Translation of: Caillou et la grande glissade.
Originally issued in series: Backpack Collection. [2001].
For children aged 3 and up.
Co-published by: Chouette Publishing and Cookie Jar Entertainment.
ISBN 978-2-89450-648-6

1. Fear - Juvenile literature. I. Cookie Jar Entertainment Inc. II. Title.
III. Series: Abracadabra (Chouette Pub.).
BF723.F4B4213 2008   j155.4'1246   C2007-941729-9

We acknowledge the financial support of the Government of Canada (Book Publishing Industry Development Program (BPIDP)) and the Government of Quebec (Tax credit for book publishing (SODEC)) for our publishing activities.

Printed in China
10 9 8 7 6 5 4 3 2 1